Cows Can't Jump

By Dave Reisman
Illustrations By Jason A. Maas

Published by Jumping Cow Press
info@jumpingcowpress.com

For Isaac, Rachel, Eli & Emma
With love,
DR

Published by Jumping Cow Press
info@jumpingcowpress.com

Printed in China

Designed by Chad Tomlinson

Cows can't jump...

...but they can swim.

Gorillas can't swim ...

...but they can swing.

Giraffes
can't swing...

...but they can gallop.

Snakes can't gallop...

...but they can slither.

...but they can stampede.

Kangaroos can't stampede...

...but they can hop.

Turtles can't hop...

...but they can dive.

Bats can't dive...

...but they can fly.

Pigs can't fly...

...but they can wallow.

Cats can't wallow...

...but they can pounce.

Fish can't pounce...

...but they
can spring.

Ducks can't spring...

...but they can waddle.

Lizards can't trample...

...but they can leap.

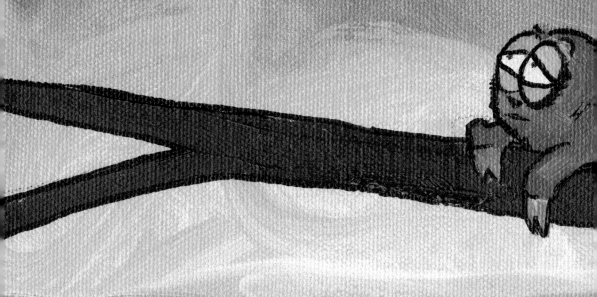

Sloths can't leap...

Mice can't waddle...

Horses can't scurry...

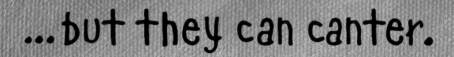

...but they can canter.

Squirrels can't canter...

...but they can glide.

Raccoons can't glide...

...but they can climb.

Elephants
can't climb...

...but they can trample.

...but they can sleep.